THE RIVER

BETWEEN

US

The River Between Us

Copyright © 2025 Emily DenOuden
All rights reserved.

No part of this book may be reproduced, stored in a retrieval system, or transmitted in any form or by any means—electronic, mechanical, photocopying, recording, or otherwise—without the prior written permission of the publisher, except for brief quotations in critical reviews or articles. This is a work of fiction. Names, characters, places, and incidents are the product of the author's imagination or used fictitiously. Any resemblance to actual persons, living or dead, or actual events is purely coincidental.

Published by Emily DenOuden

ISBN: 979-8-3009-6082-7

Cover Design: Emily DenOuden

Editing: Emily DenOuden

First Edition

For my daughter,

You are the inspiration that brought this story to life. Every word here was written for you, a glimpse into a past shaped by courage, strength, and love. These same qualities, I see in you every day.

You carry within you the legacies of two rich worlds, Indigenous and African, and with them, the stories of ancestors who walked the earth with wisdom and strength, even in the face of hardship. This book is my way of sharing one of their many stories with you. They endured so much, not only for themselves but for all of us, so that we might live with greater freedom and dignity. Their voices echo through these pages, reminding us why we stand tall and hold fast to our beliefs. Remember, my love, that life may not always be fair, but we can choose to meet it with kindness and strength. Just as Nia's mother told her, no one can take away who you are.

Your roots are strong, grounding you no matter where you go. Value what truly matters, the way Aiyana's family cherished the land. And like Aiyana and Nia, seek friendships and love that lift you up and help you grow. As you grow, may this story instill in you a deep pride in who you are and where you come from. Feel the power of the history you carry within you, the courage to rise, the love to endure, and the unwavering strength to face the world with your head held high. You are part of something beautiful,
something unbreakable,
and something that no one can ever take from you.

With all my love and hope,
Mom

The River Keeps Its Secrets, But Only From Those Unwilling To Listen...

the River Between us

Long ago, in a time when the winds carried whispers of change and the earth seemed to tremble beneath the weight of history, two young girls were born into a world that didn't always treat its children kindly.

The first was Nia.

Nia's family came from far across the ocean, from a place where the sun kissed the land and the rhythm of drums echoed in the heart of the village. But the beauty of her homeland was a distant memory, passed down in the quiet, broken voice of her mother.

Nia's mother had been taken— ripped from the warmth of her family's embrace, and brought to a land where she was no longer seen as a person, but as property. She worked from sunrise to sunset, her hands calloused and worn, in fields that stretched endlessly beneath the sky. Nia, a quiet but observant girl, grew up in the shadow of this hardship. She often sat by the window of their small cabin, listening to her mother's stories about Africa, trying to imagine a world where her people were free.

the River Between us

In the same land, but in a different world altogether, there was Aiyana.

Her people had walked the earth long before anyone else had come, knowing the secrets of every tree, every river, every mountain. They had stories that reached back to the beginning of time, carried like the wind through the generations.

the River Between us

Aiyana's family lived in harmony with the land, their feet always moving lightly on the earth, never taking more than what was needed. Aiyana, with her bright eyes and quick smile, had spent her early years learning the language of the woods, the songs of the birds, and the ancient wisdom of her people. She knew the feel of the earth beneath her bare feet, the scent of rain on pine, and the taste of fresh berries picked under a warm sun.

the River Between us

The world, however, was changing
The land Aiyana's family had tended for centuries was no longer theirs to keep.
Strangers had come, building houses and fences, and taking what they wanted without asking. Aiyana's family watched in silence as the land they loved was carved away
piece
by piece.

Nia and Aiyana's paths crossed one fateful afternoon by a river, where the sun danced on the water, unaware of the struggles that surrounded it. Nia had been sitting in the shade of an old tree, clutching a simple doll her mother had sewn from scraps of fabric. Her feet dangled over the edge of the bank, and her eyes followed the flow of the river, wondering where it went. She often sat here, away from the watchful eyes of the people in the big house, finding a moment of peace beside the running water.

It was then that she noticed a girl her age, sitting not far away on the opposite side of the river. The girl, dressed in clothes made from soft deerskin, was busy arranging smooth stones into a circle. Nia hesitated, unsure if she should speak. But something in the way the girl moved—so calm—and sure of herself, made Nia feel curious.

"Hello," Nia said quietly, her voice barely carrying across the water.

The girl looked up, her dark hair catching the light of the setting sun. She didn't seem surprised by Nia's presence, as if she had known she was there all along. A small smile crept onto her face. "Hello," she replied, her voice warm like a summer breeze. "I'm Aiyana. What's your name?"

Nia shifted nervously but felt the girl's kindness reach her. "I'm Nia."

Aiyana tilted her head slightly, still smiling.

"Do you want to come play?"

the River Between us

From that day on, the two girls became fast friends. They didn't need many words to understand each other, as if something deeper—some shared sense of the world's unfairness—connected them. Aiyana taught Nia the secrets of the forest. Together, they would weave delicate bracelets from sweet grass and leaves, their fingers nimble as they created patterns only they understood. Aiyana showed Nia how to read the river's signs, to know when rain was coming by the way the birds flew overhead, and how to find the sweetest berries hidden in the shade of the trees.

the River Between us

In return, Nia shared the stories her mother had told her. These were stories that had traveled with her family across oceans and through countless hardships. Nia's favorites were the ones about animals that talked, lions and hares who could outsmart even the strongest enemies. As she spoke, Aiyana listened closely, her eyes wide with wonder, for these stories were unlike anything she had ever heard before. The two girls would often sit together by the riverbank, their laughter mingling with the sounds of the water as they shared tales of worlds both real and imagined.

As the days passed, their bond grew stronger, like the roots of the trees that surrounded them. Nia and Aiyana were not just friends; they became each other's escape. In each other's company, they found a sense of belonging that made the world feel a little less heavy. They would hold hands as they ran barefoot through the fields, their laughter bubbling up as if the weight of the world couldn't touch them.

the River Between us

In those moments, they were free...
two girls whose friendship transcended the hardships they faced, bound not by what was happening around them, but by the pure joy they found in each other. Their friendship wasn't just about sharing stories or playing by the river; it was a lifeline, a reminder that even in the most difficult times, they could still find light.

Yet, beneath the surface of their joyful afternoons, both girls knew that life was changing in ways they could not control. The people who had taken Nia's mother from her home were the same people who were now taking Aiyana's land. Every day, Aiyana's family lost more of the land they had cared for so lovingly. And every day, Nia's mother returned from the big house, her back bent and her hands rougher than they had been the day before.

the River Between us

Then, one day, Aiyana's family began to pack their things.

"They're making us leave," Aiyana said, her voice barely a whisper. The light in her eyes had dimmed, and her shoulders slumped as she sat beside Nia at the river's edge. "This land has always been ours. I don't understand why they can take it."

the River Between us

Nia felt her heart tighten in her chest.

"That's not fair," she said softly, her voice trembling with the weight of the truth. "This is your home."

Aiyana nodded, tears glistening in her eyes. "It's all I've ever known."

the River Between us

For a moment, the two girls sat in silence, the river running quietly beside them as if it too, mourned what was being lost. Nia wanted to help, to say something that would make everything right, but she knew that the world was not always kind to those who deserved kindness. Her own mother, despite her strength, could not change the way things were.

One evening, as the sun set and the sky turned shades of orange and pink, Nia's mother found the two girls sitting together, their faces etched with sadness. She knelt beside them, her hands rough but her voice gentle. "I know it feels like everything is being taken from you," she said, looking first at Aiyana, then at her own daughter. "And it isn't fair. But you must remember that no one can take away who you are."

Aiyana wiped a tear from her cheek and looked up at Nia's mother. "But they're taking our land," she whispered, her voice small.

Nia's mother nodded slowly. "Yes, they are. But your land lives inside you, too. It lives in the stories you've learned, in the love you share with your family, and in the way you care for the earth. That can never be taken, no matter where you go."

the River Between us

Nia and Aiyana looked at each other, something unspoken passing between them. Though the world outside might be falling apart.

they still had their friendship. It was a small thing...

perhaps,

in the grand scheme of life, but it was something no one could take from them.

the River Between us

Before Aiyana's family left, she gave Nia a small, smooth stone from the river, the one they had played by so often. "So you'll remember me," Aiyana said, her voice filled with both sadness and hope.

Nia smiled through her tears and handed Aiyana a woven bracelet made from sweet grass. "And this is so you'll remember me."

They hugged each other tightly, holding on to the warmth of their friendship for as long as they could. And even though they knew their paths might not cross again for a long time, they also knew that they would carry each other in their hearts, wherever life took them.

Nia and Aiyana's families were forced to move to new places, but the stories, love, and wisdom they had shared stayed with them. They grew up strong, just like their mothers, and never forgot the lessons they had learned. They passed those lessons down to their children, and their children passed them down again, until one day, a girl named Keilani would hear these very stories and know that her own strength came from those who had come before her.

The end.